George Brown, CLASS CLOWN

Dance Your Pants Off!

For my grandparents, who always
believed I could—NK

For Asa—new little human being and nephew—AB

visit us at www.abdopublishing.com

Reinforced library bound edition published in 2014 by Spotlight, a division of the ABDO
Group, PO Box 398166, Minneapolis, MN 55439. Spotlight produces high-quality reinforced
library bound editions for schools and libraries. Published by agreement with Grosset &
Dunlap, a division of Penguin Young Readers Group.

Printed in the United States of America, North Mankato, Minnesota.
102013
012014
 This book contains at least 10% recycled materials.

Library of Congress Cataloging-in-Publication Data
This title was previously cataloged with the following information:

Krulik, Nancy E.
  Dance your pants off! / by Nancy Krulik ; illustrated by Aaron Blecha.
  p. cm. -- (George Brown, Class Clown)
  Summary: George and his classmates are excited to learn that their teacher, Mrs. Kelly, will
appear on a televised dance show, but when they go to see a taping, the Super Burp proves it is
not camera-shy.
  [1. Behavior--Fiction. 2. Belching--Fiction. 3. Dance--Fiction. 4. Reality television
programs--Fiction. 5. Schools--Fiction. 6. Magic--Fiction.] I. Title. II Series.
  PZ7.K9416 Dan 2013
  [Fic]--dc23   2012012897

ISBN 978-1-61479-216-1 (Reinforced Library Bound Edition)

George Brown, CLASS CLOWN

Dance Your Pants Off!

by Nancy Krulik
illustrated by Aaron Blecha

Grosset & Dunlap
An Imprint of Penguin Group (USA) Inc.

Chapter 1

"Let me go!"

George Brown started squirming all around. But no matter how much he twisted and turned, he could not wrestle himself away from the grip his best friend Alex had on him. "There's no way I'm doing *that* again!" George shouted.

"You're not leaving the rest of us here to face her," Alex said as he pulled George into the classroom. "And you can't run away from school. **You'll get in huge trouble.**"

George frowned. Alex was right. **He was stuck.** *Grrr*. What a way to start a Friday.

"I hate when Mrs. Kelly moves the desks," George's pal Julianna groaned as she walked into the room with George and Alex.

George felt the same way. Whenever their teacher moved the desks to the sides of the room, it could mean only one thing . . .

"Dancing," George, Julianna, and Alex groaned at the exact same time.

"What kind of dance do you think she's going to force on us today?" George asked. "I hope it's not another bullfight bossa nova."

George used his fingers to make horns on either side of his head. Alex waved his sweatshirt like a matador's cape, and George charged at him. Meanwhile, Julianna moved her feet back and forth in a bossa nova dance step.

"I'm guessing it's going to have

something to do with **ancient Egypt**,"
Alex said. "That's our next social studies
unit, isn't it?"

Before George could answer,
Mrs. Kelly came waltzing into the
classroom. Well, not waltzing, actually.
More like bobbing up and down and
moving her head from side to side.

But the way Mrs. Kelly was moving wasn't nearly as strange as the way she looked. **She was wearing a long black wig with bangs in the front.** The wig was on crooked, so the bangs kind of hung down one side of her face. On top of the wig, she was wearing a crown with a big snake on it.

"Ancient Egyptians sure dressed weird," George whispered to his friends.

"I wonder if they danced weird, too," Julianna added.

"*Every* dance Mrs. Kelly does is weird," Alex pointed out.

"What kind of dance did ancient Egyptians do?" George asked his friends.

"I have no idea," Julianna said. "But whatever it was, they did it a long, long time ago."

Suddenly, a really strange song began blaring from Mrs. Kelly's MP3 player.

"This was my favorite song when I was in college," she told the kids.

"That really *was* a long, long time ago," George whispered to Julianna and Alex. They both started laughing.

"You're gonna get it now," Louie whispered to George. "Mrs. Kelly takes dancing **really seriously**."

But Mrs. Kelly wasn't mad. "That's right, kids. Laugh," she said. "It's fun to dance."

George shot Louie a triumphant smile.

"Walk like an Egyptian!" Mrs. Kelly sang out along with the music. She turned to the side, stuck one arm out in front and one arm out in back. Then she started moving her head back and forth like a bobblehead doll.

George **nearly choked** holding back his laughter. Apparently people walked really weird in ancient Egypt. Of course George didn't say that out loud. Ever since he'd arrived at Edith B. Sugarman Elementary School, he was trying to be **the new, improved George**. And new, improved George didn't make fun of his teachers. No matter how bizarrely they acted.

"Come on, everyone, do the *'Walk Like an Egyptian'* dance with me!" Mrs. Kelly urged the class.

Dance? That didn't look like any dance George had seen anyone do before. It didn't look like *anything* he'd ever seen anyone do before.

Mrs. Kelly danced over to him.

She moved her head back and forth, and her wig slipped a little farther down the side of her head. *"Walk like an Egyptian,"* she sang out again.

George had no choice. He started bobbing his head back and forth and wiggling his hips. The next thing he knew, Sage was wiggling around beside him. *Oh man.* George hated dancing. And he didn't like Sage too much, either. So dancing with Sage was **double rotten**.

None of the kids looked too happy. But they were stuck, and they knew it. One by one they started dancing around the room with their arms pointing back and forth and their heads shaking.

"Phew! That was fun!" Mrs. Kelly exclaimed when the song finished. She pulled a tissue out from her sleeve and wiped away the **big globs of sweat that had formed on her forehead**. "What a great way to start our study of ancient Egypt."

"Are we going to learn about the pyramids?" Sage asked Mrs. Kelly. "My father says pyramids are magical."

"You will definitely get a chance to study the pyramids," Mrs. Kelly assured her.

"And the pharaohs and hieroglyphic picture writing. I know you're going to love it. And I want to hear all about what you've learned **when I get back to school**."

That surprised everyone.

"Where are you going?" Sage asked.

Mrs. Kelly gave her a big, gummy smile. **"I'm going to be dancing on TV!"**

"How long will you be gone?" Alex asked.

"Well, that depends on how well I do," Mrs. Kelly answered. "It's a brand-new dance contest show. As long as I'm not voted off the show, I will be spending my days in the Beaver Brook Ballet Studio practicing my routines. I start rehearsals tomorrow. **The first show is on at eight Monday night.** I hope you'll all watch!"

Wow. George could hardly believe what he was hearing. Mrs. Kelly dancing on TV! He really had to hand it to her. She might not have any dancing talent, but she sure had guts!

The kids were still buzzing about Mrs. Kelly when they walked into the cafeteria at lunchtime.

"We have a teacher who's going to be a TV star!" Sage said. "This is so exciting."

"I wonder how long she will stay on the show," Julianna said.

George didn't think it would be very long. Mrs. Kelly loved to dance, but she wasn't all that good at it. The judges would probably vote her off the first night. But he didn't say that. The new, improved George tried hard not to say mean things.

"Hey, check out the lunch today," Julianna said, interrupting George's thoughts. She pointed to the big board behind the lunch counter. "Flat bread, lentil pottage, and sunbaked chicken legs. What's **pottage**?"

"Maybe it's that gooey stew thing," Alex said, pointing.

George peered over the counter at some brownish glop with little lentils in it. **It looked disgusting.** Not that it mattered. Even if George put some on his tray, there would be no way to eat it. Someone had taken away all the knives, forks, and spoons.

"Anybody see the silverware?" George asked.

Just then, Mrs. Crumb, the lunch lady, appeared behind the lunch counter. She was wearing an Egyptian snake crown over her hairnet. "This is an ancient Egyptian banquet," she explained. "Ancient Egyptians ate with their hands."

"I'm glad I washed my hands after I went to the bathroom," Louie said proudly.

"Good move," Max told him.

"That's Louie, always thinking ahead," Mike agreed.

George put a bowl of **gooey lentils** and a plate with a chicken leg on his tray. He moved down toward the desserts. "What's this?" he asked Mrs. Crumb.

"Tiger nut sweets," she said.

George gulped. "You want us to eat a tiger?"

Mrs. Crumb laughed. "That's just its name, George. Actually these desserts are made of figs, walnuts, and cinnamon. They were a special treat in ancient Egypt."

George stared at the gooey brown balls. They kind of looked like what George found when he was cleaning out the cages in Mr. Furstman's pet shop.

"Try it," Mrs. Crumb said. "You're going to like it."

George doubted that. But he plopped the dessert on his tray, anyway.

George's friend Chris was already

sitting with a few other kids from his class when George and Alex arrived. Since Chris was in a different fourth-grade class, lunch was the only time during the day the boys got to see him.

"I heard music coming out of your room again this morning," Chris said. "I'm sorry."

George nodded. "Yep. Mrs. Kelly had **dance fever**."

Julianna and Sage sat down across from George, Chris, and Alex. Sage looked at her tray and sighed. "This doesn't look very delicious," she said.

George didn't know why she thought it would. Nothing they served in the school cafeteria was ever any good. Still, he was really, really hungry. Hungry enough to eat the brown slop in the bowl in front of him—if he only knew how.

"I wish I knew what I was supposed to do with the pottage stuff," George said. "I can't just scoop it up in my hands. It would slide through my fingers. And I don't want to get my new ring all covered in slop." He held up his hand so everyone could see **his new silver skull ring** on his left hand. It had bright red eyes.

"I think we're supposed to drink the pottage right from the bowl," Julianna told him.

That made sense. George lifted the bowl and took a big gulp. Slimy lentils and some sort of spicy broth **slithered down his throat**. He gagged and a couple of the lentils popped back up. *Ugh.* They didn't taste any better the second time. George put down his bowl and wiped his mouth with his sleeve.

"I can't eat this dessert," Sage complained, looking at her tray. "It makes me sick just to look at it."

George hadn't wanted to eat the tiger nut sweets, either. But if it would make Sage sick, it could be worth it. **He picked up a lumpy brown ball and took a big bite.**

"Hey! It's pretty good!" he exclaimed.

"Leave it to a kid who acts nutty to like a nut *treat*," Louie joked.

The kids all laughed—except George and Alex. They were the only ones who knew why George sometimes **acted nuts**. And it wasn't funny at all.

It started when George and his parents first moved to Beaver Brook. George's dad was in the army, so they moved around a lot. George had plenty of experience with being the new kid in school, so he'd expected the first day in his new school to stink. First days always did. But *this* first day was **the stinkiest**.

In his old school, George had been the class clown. He was always pulling pranks and making jokes. But George had promised himself that things were going to be different at Edith B. Sugarman Elementary School. No more pranks. No more squishing red Jell-O between his teeth and telling everyone it was blood. No more imitating teachers behind their backs. *No more trouble.*

The thing was, being the well-behaved kid in a new school also meant that George was the new kid with no new friends. No one at Edith B. Sugarman Elementary School seemed to even know he was alive.

After his rotten first day at his new school, George's parents took him out to

Ernie's Ice Cream Emporium to cheer him up. While they were sitting outside and George was finishing his root beer float, a shooting star flashed across the sky. So George made a wish.

I want to make kids laugh—but not get into trouble.

But the star was gone before George could finish the wish. So only half came true—*the first half.*

A minute later, George had a funny feeling in his belly. It was like there were **hundreds of tiny bubbles bouncing around** in there. The bubbles hopped up and down and all around. They ping-ponged their way into his chest and bing-bonged their way up into his throat. And then . . .

George let out a big burp. A *huge* burp. A SUPER burp! The super burp was loud, and it was *magic.*

Suddenly George **lost control** of his arms and legs. It was like they had minds of their own. His hands grabbed straws and stuck them up his nose like a walrus. His feet jumped up on the table and started dancing the hokey pokey. Everyone at Ernie's started laughing. The laughing sounded great—just like the old days. But his parents yelling at him *also* sounded like the old days.

The super burp came back lots of times after that. And every time it did: Bubble bubble, George got in trouble. Half the store owners in town got really nervous whenever George walked in. Not that he blamed them. After all, the burp had already made him destroy the paddleball display at Tyler's Toy Shop, knock down the Christmas tree at Mabel's Department Store, and toss pizza dough onto his head at the Pizza Place.

The only one of George's friends in Beaver Brook who knew about the super burp was Alex. George hadn't told Alex about the burp. He'd figured it out all by himself. Lucky for George, Alex was **a really good friend**. Not only did he keep George's gas explosion problem a secret, he was trying to come up with a cure. Too bad he hadn't been able to do that just yet.

Which meant the burp was still out there, **ready to strike** when George least expected it.

Chapter 2

"Rawk. Hello. Rawk. Hello."

Petey, the parrot that sat on a perch in the front of Mr. Furstman's pet shop, was the first one to greet George when he arrived at work on Saturday morning.

George petted the soft green feathers on the top of Petey's head and gave him a piece of apple. "Hello to you, too," he told Petey.

"Rawk. Hello," Petey answered. *Hello* was the only word he knew.

"**Hey, watch out, kid.** Don't trip over the wires!" a man shouted at George.

George looked down. There was a tangle of black cable wires

at his feet. There were bright lights and cameras all over the store.

"What's going on?" George asked Mr. Furstman.

"We're filming a commercial for the new lizard and snake section of the shop," Mr. Furstman explained. "It's going to be shown at the Beaver Brook Movie Theater."

"Oh, you mean like one of those things they show while everyone is waiting for the lights to go down?" George asked him.

"Exactly," Mr. Furstman agreed. "Anyone who goes to see a movie in this town is going to hear about our lizards and snakes."

Just then a small woman carrying a clipboard ran over to Mr. Furstman. "D. W. is ready," she said.

"Who's D. W.?" George wondered.

A tall, skinny man leaped up from a

cloth chair in the back of the shop. "Did someone just ask who D. W. is?" he demanded.

"Uh . . . yeah," George admitted.

The skinny man stared angrily at George. Then he turned to the small woman with the clipboard. "Is he kidding, Christina?" he asked her. **"How can he not know who I am?"**

"D. W. is the director of all the commercials that are played before the movies at the movie theater," Christina explained.

"NO!" D. W. bellowed. "I am the director of the Beaver Brook Movie Theater's *informative, very short films.* I'm calling this one *The Creature from the Back of the Store.* It's catchy, don't you think?"

George didn't know what to think.

D. W. pointed to the snakes and

lizards in the cages that lined the back
wall of the pet shop. "Now which of these
should be my star?" he wondered out loud.
Then he turned to Mr. Furstman. "Don't
forget, I **demand** final say on the casting
of all my films."

"I was thinking the garter snake,"
Mr. Furstman said. "Or maybe the gecko."

"Hmm . . . what do you think, kid?"
D. W. asked George.

George didn't answer. He couldn't
think about any snake or gecko. He was
more worried about what was up in his
neck-o.

There were bubbles there. Big ones.

And they were moving fast. Already they'd bing-bonged in his belly, kickboxed his kidneys, and rattled his rib cage. Now they were tickling his tonsils. Any minute now . . .

B-U-U-U-R-P!

George opened his mouth to say "excuse me." But instead, he said, "I'm ready for my close-up!" His face **plastered** itself right in front of the camera.

"Cut it out, kid!" the cameraman shouted. "Your breath is fogging up my camera lens."

George's tongue moved in and out like a snake searching for food. "*Hissss . . . ,*" he said as he looked right into the camera.

"Get that kid off my set!" D. W. demanded.

"George, *please*," Mr. Furstman said. "This isn't a good time to goof around."

But the burp thought it was the perfect time. Suddenly, George's body dropped to the ground. He began slithering around the floor on his belly.

"What do you think you're doing?" D. W. demanded.

But that was just it. *George* wasn't thinking. The burp was doing the thinking for him. And right now it was thinking it would be fun to be a snake.

"Hissss!" George's tongue slithered in and out. It **licked up some dirt** that a customer had tracked into the store.

27

Whoosh! Suddenly, George felt the air rush out of him. It was like someone had **popped a balloon** in the bottom of his belly. The super burp was gone.

But George was still there, lying on his belly, with dirt on his tongue.

"Get up!" D. W. shouted. "I'm not auditioning anyone for the role of the snake." He put his hand to his head. "I can't work in these conditions," he moaned.

"George, please . . . ," Mr. Furstman pleaded.

George jumped up and quickly moved out of the way. D. W. was already plenty annoyed. He didn't want Mr. Furstman to be mad at him, too.

D. W. pointed to a gecko who was sitting on a branch in his terrarium. "This will be the star of my film."

"**Great choice**, D. W.," Christina and the cameraman said at once.

Mr. Furstman smiled at George. "If you want to help with the commercial . . ."

"*Informative, very short film*," D. W. corrected him.

"Uh, right," Mr. Furstman said. "If you want to help with the *informative, very short film*, why don't you feed the gecko a cricket?"

"Yes, sir." George reached into **a bucket of bugs** and pulled out a nice juicy cricket for the gecko to snack on.

"Okay, everybody . . . quiet on the set!" D. W. shouted. "And . . . *action!*"

Later that afternoon, as George was walking home from work, he bumped into Julianna and Sage.

"Hi, Georgie," Sage cooed. Then she did that weird batting-her-eyelashes thing.

"Hey," George grumbled at Sage. He smiled at Julianna. **"What's up?"**

"Mrs. Kelly and some other dancers from that new show are practicing at the Beaver Brook Ballet Studio on Kukamonga Road," Julianna said. "We're heading over to **sneak a peek**."

"I take ballet lessons there," Sage said. "So I'm sure they'll let us in. You want to come with us, Georgie?"

Usually George avoided going anywhere with Sage. But he was really curious about what kind of dance Mrs. Kelly would be doing on Monday's show.

"Okay," George agreed. **"Let's go spy on Mrs. Kelly."**

A few minutes later George was inside the Beaver Brook Ballet Studio, peering through the window that separated the lobby from the room where the dancers were. Through the glass, George could see some dancers doing flying leaps across the floor. Others were twirling, and a few were bending their knees outward with their backs straight.

"Those are called *pliés*," Sage said, pointing to the bending dancers. "I can do one, Georgie. Want to see?"

No, George did *not* want to see. He wasn't there to watch Sage dance. He was there to spy on Mrs. Kelly.

He looked around the studio, searching for his teacher. And then, finally, he saw her. She was off in the corner, far from the other dancers. Instead of bending, leaping, or twirling, **Mrs. Kelly was on the ground doing somersaults**. At least George thought they were supposed to be somersaults. It was hard to tell because every time she flipped over, Mrs. Kelly would **tip to the side**.

"We never do anything like *that* in dance class," Sage said.

George watched as Mrs. Kelly **tucked her head between her legs** and started to turn over again. But this time she didn't flip or flop. She just stayed there. **Stuck.** *With her rear end high up in the air.*

"Oh man, I can't watch this anymore," George said as he turned away from the window. "No guy should ever have to see his teacher's rear end looking like that. Not ever."

Chapter 3

"I'm telling you, dudes, when Mrs. Kelly gets on that stage, it's not gonna be pretty," George told Alex, Julianna, and Chris as they walked into the movie theater on Sunday to see *The Monster That Menaced Milwaukee.*

"She was **that bad**?" Alex asked.

"*Worse* than bad," Julianna said.

"I'm going to have **nightmares about her rear end** for months," George added.

Alex shook his head. "I don't want Mrs. Kelly to be embarrassed on TV. She's a nice teacher. She's just a little . . ."

"Different?" George said.

"Exactly," Alex agreed.

Chris stopped at the middle row in the theater. "These seats okay?" he asked.

George shrugged. The only problem with the seats was that Louie, Mike, and Max were two rows ahead of them.

"You're sure Mr. Furstman's commercial is going to be shown today?" Chris asked George.

"Yeah. D. W. said it would be ready for today," George said. "**Informative, very short films** take a very short time to make."

Louie turned around and glared at George. "No one's here to watch the commercials. They're here to see *The Monster That Menaced Milwaukee*."

"Yeah, I want to see the monster," Max said.

"I want to see Milwaukee," Mike added.

Just then a picture of Mr. Furstman's pet shop flashed on the screen. "This is it!" George said excitedly.

"It came from the back of the store . . . and it was hungry!" a booming voice shouted. A picture of a gecko appeared on the giant screen. It opened its mouth and **swallowed a cricket, whole**.

"Hey, George!" Chris exclaimed as he pointed at the screen. "That's your hand. I can tell because **that's your ring**!"

Sure enough, George's hand and his skull ring could be seen holding the cricket up for the gecko to grab.

"Cool, dude," Alex said. **"You're a movie star!"**

"It's not a movie. It's just a commercial." Louie whipped around in his seat to glare at George. His popcorn went flying all over the floor.

"Now look what you did!" Louie
shouted at George.

"Me?" George asked. "What did I do?"

Louie glared at him. "I can't watch a
movie without popcorn," he insisted.

Max and Mike dropped to the floor
and started picking up the kernels.

"Don't worry," Max said. "I'll pick it
up."

"Me too," Mike said. He held up a
brown kernel. "Hey! This one's moving."

"That's not popcorn," Louie said. "It's
a **cockroach**!"

"Oh," Mike said. He looked at the

wriggling bug. "It might taste okay if you put butter on it."

"Get that thing away from me!" **Louie screeched**. He jumped up and started climbing over the seat in front of him to get away from the squirming roach. "I hate bugs!"

"Sorry," Mike said. "I forgot."

Louie turned and glared at George. "Now I have to go buy another bag of popcorn. It's a good thing my mother gave me lots of extra money. I'm going to get a giant soda while I'm at it."

As Louie skated off on his sneakers with wheels to buy popcorn and soda, George settled back into his seat. It was almost time for *The Monster That Menaced Milwaukee*. But George doubted the movie monster could be any creepier than the real-life one: Louie— The Kid Who Could Buy the World.

Chapter 4

"Oh, *Georgie*, I always knew you were a star," Sage said as the kids walked into class 401 on Monday morning. "I wish I'd been at the movie theater on Sunday so I could have seen you on the big screen."

"It was just his *hand*," Louie corrected her. "He wasn't the star of the commercial. That iguana was."

"It wasn't an iguana. It was a gecko," George told Louie. "There's a big difference. Geckos actually—"

"Whatever," Louie interrupted. "The point is *you* weren't the star of anything."

"Hey, check it out," Alex whispered to

George. "Mr. Trainer is our substitute."

George looked toward the front of the classroom. Sure enough, **his gym teacher** was standing by the board. This was going to be weird. Gym teachers never knew anything about school stuff; they only knew about gym stuff.

"Okay, let's get to work," Mr. Trainer said. "Mrs. Kelly left me instructions to start teaching you about ancient Egypt in social studies today. Can anyone tell me what you have learned so far?"

Louie's hand shot up first. "We know how to walk like Egyptians." He put his arms in front and in back of himself and bobbed his head back and forth. "Like this."

Mr. Trainer gave Louie a strange look. **"That's unique,"** he said.

George laughed. When grown-ups said *unique*, they usually meant *odd*. And odd was exactly how Louie looked.

"Mrs. Kelly said we'd be learning about the pyramids soon," Sage added.

"Well, I don't know a whole lot about pyramids," Mr. Trainer admitted. "But I do know about phys ed. **So let's go down to the gym and have our social studies lesson there.**"

"They had gym class in ancient Egypt?" Julianna asked as the kids headed out of the classroom and down the hall to the gym.

"Not exactly," Mr. Trainer answered. "But they had games. For instance, they played handball. And archery was a huge sport. So was wrestling."

"Wrestling! Like on TV?" George asked. "I love wrestling! Did you guys see the one where Mr. Mammoth leaped off the ropes and landed right on Harry the Horrendous?"

"Mr. Mammoth is amazing," Julianna agreed. "He kept wrestling even after Harry the Horrendous **bit him on the nose**."

"Well, they didn't exactly have *that* kind of wrestling back in ancient Egypt," Mr. Trainer said. "For one thing, the wrestlers were covered in oil."

"Gross," Sage said. "You're not going to make us cover ourselves in oil, are you?"

Mr. Trainer shook his head. "We're not wrestling today. We're going to play handball." He picked up a pink rubber ball. "Let me explain the rules. We start by bouncing the ball . . ."

George didn't pay attention to the rest of the handball rules. He couldn't. He was too busy paying attention to the bouncing that was going on inside his belly. **The super burp was back!** And it really wanted to come out and play. Already the bubbles had bing-bonged past his belly and cling-clanged over his colon.

George clamped his mouth shut and tried to keep the bubbles from bursting out of him. **But the bubbles were strong!** They twisted and turned between his teeth, licked at his lips, and then . . .

George let out a burp that was so loud it could have **shaken the pyramids**.

George opened his mouth to say "excuse me," but instead he shouted, "I'm George the Giant Wrestling Superstar."

Then George's body took a flying leap . . . and landed right on top of Louie!

"What the?!" Louie exclaimed as George's elbow pounded right into his gut and knocked him to the ground.

"I'm George the Giant Wrestling Superstar!" George told Louie.

"Dude, no!" Alex shouted.

Dude, yes. The burp was **rarin' to wrestle**.

"George! I said we *weren't* wrestling today," Coach Trainer told him. "We're playing handball."

But the burp didn't want to play handball. It wanted to flip Louie over onto his belly.

"The Boston Crab!" George shouted as his arms grabbed Louie's legs.

Louie had been caught by surprise. But as soon as he caught his breath, he shouted, "You can't outwrestle me, you weirdo freak." He reached out his arm and tripped George. Now both boys were on the floor.

"Boys, get up!" Coach Trainer shouted.

George wanted to get up. He really did. But he couldn't. George wasn't in charge

THE BOSTON CRAB!

anymore. The burp was. And it wanted to put Louie in a half nelson.

"Ahh! Gotcha!" George shouted as he grabbed Louie under the armpit. *Yuck!* It was **wet, sweaty, and stinky** under there. But the burp didn't care. Burps love sweat and stink.

"No, you don't!" Louie shouted, slipping from George's grip and flipping him on his back.

"Go, Louie!" Max and Mike shouted.

Mr. Trainer reached over and tried to pull the boys apart. George's elbow whacked him in the face.

"Oh! My nose!" Coach Trainer exclaimed.

"Dude, stop!" Alex yelled.

But George *couldn't* stop. He rolled over and flipped Louie. Now George was on top.

Then Louie flipped George. Louie was on top.

Then George was on top.
Then Louie.
George.
Louie.
George.
Louie.

Pop! Suddenly, George felt all the air rush out of him. The super burp was gone. But George was still there. And Louie still had him **pinned to the floor**.

"I'm the champion!" Louie declared.

"Lou-ie! Lou-ie! Lou-ie!" Max and Mike chanted.

"Boys, get up!" Mr. Trainer shouted angrily.

"He started it," Louie insisted.

George knew that wasn't true. The super burp had started it. But George didn't say that. Instead he opened his mouth to say "I'm sorry." And that was exactly what came out.

Mr. Trainer shook his head. "George, wrestling can be dangerous if you don't know what you're doing. You and I will have a long talk about this—**during recess**."

George frowned. He was in trouble

again. And there was no way he could wrestle his way out of it. The super burp had George in **a rope-hung figure-four armlock**. And it wasn't letting go.

Chapter 5

"That burp really messed me up big-time," George **groaned** as he sat down next to Alex in the cafeteria at lunchtime. "Louie's never going to let me forget I lost a wrestling match against him."

"Yeah, that was a tough break," Alex said. "Who knew he had moves like that?"

"And to top it all off, I have to spend recess with Mr. Trainer," George added. "He said he's giving me extra homework, too. I hope I can get it done before Mrs. Kelly's dance show comes on. I'm not allowed to watch TV until all my work is finished."

"That stinks," Alex agreed.

"There has to be a way to get rid

of this troublemaking burp," George whispered.

Alex grinned. He pulled a huge container of cut-up, yellow-orange–colored fruit from his lunch bag.

"What's that?" George asked him.

"Papaya," Alex answered. "I was reading on The Burp No More Blog that eating lots of papaya is good for your digestion. The only other cure I saw posted was to **make sure your false teeth are tightly sealed to your gums**. You don't have false teeth, do you?"

George grinned so Alex could see his teeth. "They're all mine," he said.

"Papaya it is," Alex agreed.

George put a piece of papaya in his mouth and started to chew. It was slimy and mealy, but at least it tasted better than the spicy mustard cure Alex had him try a few weeks ago. The mustard made George feel like **a fire-breathing dragon**. And it didn't work, which meant George wound up more like a fire-*burping* dragon.

"So long, *loser*," Louie said as he, Max, and Mike walked past George on the way to the school yard. "Too bad you're spending recess with Mr. Trainer. We could have wrestled some more. I have a few moves I didn't get to show you. We're gonna play **killer ball** at recess instead. Of course, *you're* going to miss it. Bummer for you."

Killer ball was a game Louie had made up. It was like dodgeball, only meaner. George wasn't sorry he was missing that game. He wasn't sorry to be missing Louie's wrestling moves, either. The only move Louie could do that would make George happy was to move far, *far* away. Because there just wasn't enough room in Beaver Brook for both of them.

"George! It's for you!" his mother shouted later that evening while George was busy typing the third paragraph of his essay **"Why I Shouldn't Fool Around in the Gym."** George hit Save on his computer and ran for the hall phone.

"Hey, dude," Alex said. "I'm just checking on how **the papaya cure** is working."

"Well . . . ," George said slowly.

"Did you burp?" Alex asked.

"No," George told him. "But . . ."

"But what?" Alex said. "It's been hours since you ate all that papaya. And you haven't burped. So it's a cure."

"Maybe, but it's a pain, too," George said.

"Why?"

"Well, you know how you said it was good for my digestion?" George asked.

"Yeah, that's the point," Alex said.

"Well, it's really good," George said. "*Too* good. I've been **in and out of the bathroom** all afternoon long. The papaya makes you go—a lot!"

"Oh," Alex said. **"That's a problem."**

"Tell me about it," George said. "Do you know how hard it is to do your homework when you have to stop every five minutes to go to the bathroom? And it *really* stinks in there now." George paused for a minute. "I gotta go," he told Alex.

"To do your homework?" Alex asked.

"No," George said. "I mean I gotta *go*. It's the papaya . . . again."

George didn't wait for Alex to say

good-bye. He just hung up the phone and **ran for the bathroom**. It was gonna be a long night.

Ping!

A little while later, just as George was finishing his essay, the e-mail alert on his computer sounded. The e-mail was from Louie. It said:

Check out this way-cool webcast. It's what everyone's going to be talking about at school tomorrow.

George was definitely curious. He clicked the link that Louie had sent him.

"Welcome to *Life with Louie!*" the computer shouted as Louie appeared on the screen, sitting at his kitchen table and smiling for the camera.

"This is the show that's **all Louie, all the time**!" Louie announced. "I'm the star of this show. All of me. *Not just my hand.*"

George frowned. He knew Louie had said that **especially for him**.

"Tonight for dinner, I am having steak, broccoli, and a baked potato," Louie continued. "Let me show you how perfectly my personal chef has cooked this steak." Louie picked up his knife and began to cut the steak.

George rolled his eyes. Why would anyone want to watch this?

"Hey, get a shot of how I chew with my mouth closed," Louie shouted to his off-screen cameraman.

George laughed. Louie might have known how to chew with his mouth closed, but right now he was talking with his mouth *full*. **Bits of Louie's chewed-up meat were being broadcast all over the Internet.**

The camera started shaking. A pair of blue sneakers appeared on the screen.

"Hey! You're supposed to be filming *me*," Louie shouted. "Not your feet."

"Oops, sorry," George heard Max say off-camera. "I had to scratch." Max shifted the camera and started filming Louie again.

"You're not supposed to talk!" Louie yelled, showing off the chewed meat bits that were stuck to his tongue.

"How about I film you putting butter on your potato?" Max asked. "I could back up a little and get your whole plate on the screen and—"

"Watch where you're walking!" Louie shouted at him. "You're gonna trip over that stool and—"

CRASH!

The picture went blank. But the sound was still working. George heard Louie shouting. "Look what you did! You spilled my chocolate milk all over my broccoli. Why would I want to eat **chocolate broccoli**?"

George started laughing. *Life with Louie* was actually pretty funny.

A second later, Louie was back on the screen. He looked the same except now he had a big chocolate-milk stain on his shirt and a piece of broccoli in his hair.

"Follow me into the bathroom," Louie told Max. "I'm going to wash my hands." He smiled at the camera. "Did you know that you are supposed to wash for as long as it takes for you to sing 'Happy Birthday'? I sing every time I wash. So you guys are in for a real treat . . ."

Just then, George's dad called to him from the living room. "Son, it's eight o'clock. Did you finish all your work?"

George clicked off Louie's webcast. **Mrs. Kelly's big dance debut** was about to hit the screen. And there was no way George was missing *that*.

Chapter 6

"Welcome to *Dance Your Pants Off!*" the TV announcer said cheerfully. "I'm **Guy Smirks**. This is the new show where local dancing stars compete for a ten-thousand-dollar prize and the *Dance Your Pants Off* championship crown." The studio audience began to cheer.

George frowned. He wouldn't exactly call Mrs. Kelly a dancing *star*.

"Our first contestant is from nearby Beaver Brook," Guy Smirks continued. "She's a fourth-grade teacher at Edith B. Sugarman Elementary School. **Please welcome Mildred Kelly!**"

Mildred? George started to laugh. He'd always figured that Mrs. Kelly had a first name—and that it couldn't be *Mrs.* But *Mildred?*

Mrs. Kelly had done some strange dances in school—there was that "Walk Like an Egyptian" thing they did the other day and the alley cat and even a hula. But tonight's dance was stranger than all of them put together.

Mrs. Kelly flung her arms up in the air and stood stick straight. She kicked her leg in front of her and started wiggling her hips all over the place. Then she turned around so her rear end was to the audience, bent over, and peeked between her legs.

"This is just embarrassing," George said with a groan.

"Mrs. Kelly does have a *unique* dance style," his mother said.

"I've never seen anything like it," his dad agreed.

George laughed.

Mrs. Kelly did a somersault, then finished off her dance with a split. Well, sort of a split. Her back leg was bent instead of straight.

"That was **interesting**," Guy Smirks said as Mrs. Kelly struggled to her feet. "Let's see whether the judges will put you through to the next round."

"I think Mrs. Kelly will be back in school tomorrow," George said. "No way any of the judges liked that."

"Mildred, that was very **unique choreography**," the first judge, some man named Anthony, said. "Where did you study dance?"

"Well, I'm not exactly a trained dancer," Mrs. Kelly told him. "I just dance what I feel."

"Dance is about a feeling," the second judge, a small woman named Lily, said. "I remember once when I was dancing on the stage in Boise, Idaho, I started to change the choreography right in the middle of the performance **because I felt something**."

"Something in the music?" Guy Smirks asked her.

"No, something on my arm," Lily said. "A fly. I decided to try and swat it. For the rest of the dance I chased that fly around the stage. I never caught him, though."

"I thought Mildred's dance was fascinating," the third judge, an English guy named Cecil, said. He was nearly **jumping out of his seat with excitement**. "I vote to bring you back."

"I do, too," Lily, the fly-swatting dancer judge, agreed.

"I'll make it three," Anthony said. "We'll see you Thursday night."

George stared at the TV. The judges were sending Mrs. Kelly through to the next round after seeing that dance? How was it even possible?

"Did you see that last night?" Alex asked as George walked into the schoolyard on Tuesday morning.

"Oh yeah," George said. "And I couldn't believe it."

Just then, Louie came rolling over on his sneakers with wheels. "My webcast *was* awesome, wasn't it?"

"We were talking about Mrs. Kelly on *Dance Your Pants Off*," George told Louie.

Louie frowned. "Why is everybody talking about that show? There are a million dance-contest shows on TV. But there's only one webcast that stars *me*."

"Yes, but *Dance Your Pants Off* is the only dance show that our teacher was on,"

Julianna reminded Louie. "That was one strange dance," she added, turning to her friends.

"I can't believe you all turned off my webcast to watch Mrs. Kelly," Louie continued. "You missed me doing my long division."

"Yeah," Mike said. "And that was a really interesting thing to watch. Louie is great at long division."

"Definitely," Max agreed. "He only missed the answer by two. **That's real close.**"

George, Alex, Sage, and Julianna ignored Louie and his two Echoes.

"It would be cool if Mrs. Kelly won," Julianna said. "We'd be the only kids in the whole world to have a champion dancer for a teacher."

"We'd be famous," Sage added. "Sort of, anyway."

"Yeah, but do you really think she has a chance?" George asked.

"Last night the judges kept her alive. But now it's up to the people watching the show to vote for who they think danced best," Alex said. "And I'm not sure too many of them will vote for Mrs. Kelly . . . *unless* we help her," he added with a smile.

George knew that smile. He'd seen it before. Alex was coming up with a plan.

"How can we do that?" Chris asked.

"We could start **a campaign to get people to vote for Mrs. Kelly**," Alex suggested.

"That's a great idea!" Julianna agreed. "I could talk about Mrs. Kelly on my sports segment during morning announcements."

"Yeah," George said. "And we could make posters and put them up all over town."

"I bet everyone around here would help," Alex said.

"Yeah!" Max added.

"*You* can't help," Louie told Max. "You and Mike are going to be very busy helping me with my next *Life with Louie* webcast. It's going to be amazing. I'm going to show everyone my complete collection of **fungus trading cards**. You can buy them in the gift shop at the Beaver Brook Science Center. Each picture is of a fungus you can find at the Farley Family Fungus Room."

George laughed. Louie was always bragging about the room his family had donated to the museum. He was really into fungi. Which made sense, since Louie was kind of like a fungus—annoying and really, really hard to get rid of.

74

Chapter 7

"So don't forget to watch *Dance Your Pants Off* tomorrow night and vote for our own Mrs. Kelly!" Julianna said into the camera during Wednesday's morning announcements. "Let's make Edith B. Sugarman Elementary School **famous**!"

Louie looked at the closed-circuit TV in the classroom and frowned. "That's not fair," he said. "How come Julianna gets to pick which shows to tell kids to watch?"

"Maybe because it's *her* sports broadcast," George said.

"Dancing's not a sport," Louie insisted.

"It is the way Mrs. Kelly does it," Sage

said. "She kicks her leg like in soccer. She **wiggles her rear end** like a batter at the plate in baseball. And she jumps up in the air like a basketball player taking a shot."

"I never saw any basketball player land in a split," George whispered to Alex.

Alex laughed. "You crack me up, dude," he said.

But Mr. Trainer wasn't cracking up. "Is something funny, you guys?" he asked George and Alex.

George stopped laughing. He was still trying to be the new and improved George. And that meant no more jokes about his teacher.

"There's something to what Sage is saying," Mr. Trainer told the kids. "Lots of athletes take dance classes to learn to move better. Boxers and football players take ballet, for instance."

George imagined a big football player

dancing around in ballet shoes. It made him start to laugh all over again. But he stopped really quickly after Mr. Trainer gave him a look.

"Now that the announcements are over, let's get to work," Mr. Trainer told the class. "I think today we will start with math."

Mr. Trainer taped a poster with seven pictures on it to the board. The first five pictures just looked like **whirls and squiggles**, while the sixth one was of a frog, and the last one was of a man sitting on his knees.

"What does this have to do with math?" Louie asked Mr. Trainer.

"These are the **hieroglyphic picture words** that the ancient Egyptians used for numbers," Mr. Trainer explained.

George thought about asking Louie if he was going to use those pictures to do long division on his webcast.

But he stopped himself. George thought it was pretty funny thinking about Louie being wrong by just a frog and a squiggle.

But he had a feeling Louie and Mr. Trainer wouldn't agree. And George didn't want any **extra homework** tonight. There was way too much to do after school.

"Hi, Mom!" George greeted his mother as he walked into her craft store, the Knit Wit, after school.

"Hi, honey," George's mom said. She looked up from the register and smiled at Julianna, Alex, Sage, and Chris. "Hi, kids."

"Hello," Julianna, Alex, Sage, and Chris all said at once.

"Do you mind if we put this sign in the store window?" George asked. He held

up a piece of paper. It had a drawing of
Mrs. Kelly on it and said:

"That's a great sign," George's mom
said.

"Chris drew it," George told her
proudly. "He's an **amazing artist**."

"It wasn't a big deal," Chris insisted.
"Mrs. Kelly's easier to draw than a
superhero. She doesn't wear a cape or
tights."

"Let's hope not," Alex said.

George had to agree with that. **Mrs. Kelly in tights** was definitely *not* something he wanted to see on TV—or anywhere else for that matter.

Julianna taped the sign to the store window. "Okay, guys, come on," she said. "We have to put these things up all over town."

"Thanks, Mom," George called as the kids got ready to leave.

"No problem," she answered. "I'll see you at home for dinner."

"Where should we go next?" Julianna asked. "Tyler's Toy Shop?"

"How about the Pizza Palace?" Chris suggested. "I'm starving."

George frowned. He'd had some really bad burp attacks in both of those places.

"How about I take a sign to Mr. Furstman's pet shop, since I work there?" George suggested. Mr. Furstman never seemed to get mad at anything the burp made George do.

"I'll go with you," Alex said. "And after that we can go to Mr. Stubbs's Barbershop."

"Sounds like a plan," Julianna said. "Chris and I can go to Mabel's Department Store after we stop at the pizzeria. We'll cover a lot more ground if we **split up into teams**. What do you want to do, Sage?"

"I'm going with *Georgie*," Sage said, doing that creepy blinking-her-eyelashes thing again. "Maybe you could show me how you fed that gecko, since I didn't get to see your commercial at the theater."

George looked to Alex for help.

"No time for that," Alex said. "We have a lot of signs to post."

"Okay. Then I can come by the store on Saturday when you're working and you can show me then," Sage said.

Grrr. Sage was as annoying as the super burp. And almost as hard to get rid of.

"Hi, Mr. Stubbs," Alex greeted the barber as he, George, and Sage walked into his shop a little while later.

George loved Mr. Stubbs's Barbershop. There were two barber chairs set up facing the mirror. On the shelf were scissors and combs for haircuts and shaving cream and razors for giving shaves. Best of all, by the window there was a **pole with red, white, and blue stripes** that whirled around and around, so it looked like the stripes were moving up the pole and then down again.

"Hello, Alex," Mr. Stubbs said. "Are you here for a trim?"

Alex shook his head. "Nope. We're here to help Mrs. Kelly."

Mr. Stubbs looked around.

"Mrs. Kelly?" he asked. "Does she need a haircut? Where is she?"

"Dancing," Sage said. "On TV. And **she needs your help**."

Mr. Stubbs seemed very confused. "*My* help? I can't dance. I've got two left feet."

George looked down at Mr. Stubbs's feet. They looked pretty normal to him. One left foot and one right.

But then George noticed something totally not normal. And definitely not right. BUBBLES. And they were bing-bonging and ping-ponging all over George's belly.

The bubbles hadn't popped out since Alex had given George all that papaya two days ago. But they were back now. And they were **stronger than ever**. Already the bubbles had crisscrossed over his colon and pounced on his pancreas.

Suddenly, George remembered the special signal he and Alex had set up for when the burp was starting to bubble over. The minute Alex saw it, he was supposed to run over and get George away from where he was, before trouble could happen. George didn't always have a chance to signal to Alex before the burp burst out. But he did this time!

George rubbed his belly and patted his head. But Alex was too busy talking to Mr. Stubbs to notice.

The bubbles ricocheted off George's ribs and hip-hopped over his heart.

George patted his belly and rubbed his head. But there was still no help from Alex.

The bubbles tap-danced on George's tongue, twisted their way around his teeth, and then . . .

BUUURP!

Bubble, bubble, George was in trouble!

"Dude, no!" Alex cried out, finally noticing George.

Dude, *yes*! The super burp was free, and it wanted to play.

George opened his mouth to say "excuse me." But that's not what came out. Instead, he shouted, **"Shave and a haircut, two bits!"**

Suddenly, George's hands reached out and grabbed a can of shaving cream. *Pssshhhh.* White foam sprayed under George's nose and all over his chin.

"George, put that down!" Mr. Stubbs scolded him.

George wanted to put the shaving cream down. **He really did.** But George wasn't in charge anymore. The burp was. And it wanted a white, foamy mustache and beard.

Then George's hands aimed the spray can at Sage. *Pssshhhh.*

"Georgie, no!" Sage cried out.

Any other time, George would have thought it was pretty funny seeing Sage with shaving cream on her face and in her

86

hair. But not now. Now it was just *ba-a-ad*!

"George, put that down and get out of my shop—now!" Mr. Stubbs shouted.

George wanted his feet to run out of the store as fast as they could. But that's not what the burp wanted. **It wanted to climb up that barber pole!** And that's just what George did. The next thing anyone knew, there was red, white, blue, and George *Brown* stripes going around and around on the barber pole.

"George, get down!" Mr. Stubbs yelled. "You're going to break that."

"Wheeeee!" George's mouth shouted out. "Wheeeee!"

Whoosh! Suddenly George felt something pop in the bottom of his belly. All the air rushed out of him. The super burp was gone!

"Whoa!" George slid right off the pole. He landed with a *bam*, right on his butt. Everyone just stared at him.

George opened his mouth to say "I'm sorry." And that was exactly what came out.

Mr. Stubbs shook his head. **"What a mess,"** he said. "George, I think you'd better leave now."

George stood up and slunk out of the store. He watched through the window as Alex handed Mr. Stubbs a "Vote for Mildred Kelly" poster and Sage wiped the shaving cream from her face and hair.

George frowned and kicked at the ground. Mr. Stubbs was so angry, he might never let George in his barbershop again. George might have to start going to the **beauty salon** where his mom went. The air there smelled like perfume, and the chairs were all pink. It was no place for a kid like George.

Stupid super burp. It was making trouble for George everywhere. Before long, it wouldn't be Mrs. Kelly's face on posters all over town. It would be George's face—on a wanted poster!

Chapter 8

By Wednesday evening, it seemed as though every store in Beaver Brook had a **"Vote for Mildred Kelly"** poster in the window. There was no way anyone in town could miss seeing them. Just in case, George wanted to e-mail all the kids in the fourth grade to remind them to watch the show and vote for Mrs. Kelly!

But before George could type even one word, **a brand-new e-mail** arrived in his in-box.

Life with Louie starts in two minutes. You don't want to miss this one. Everyone's gonna be talking about it tomorrow!

Louie was wrong. George wanted to miss *Life with Louie*. He really did. But somehow he **couldn't stop himself** from clicking the link. He just had to see how Louie was going to make a jerk of himself this time.

The minute George clicked on the link, he saw Louie—dressed in a fluffy red bathrobe and wearing a clear shower cap on his head.

Oh boy, this was gonna be good!

"I love to sing in the shower," Louie said. He turned to look at his off-screen cameraman. "Max, follow me."

Louie began to walk down the hall. Max followed close behind. So close that pretty soon all you could see was the blur of Louie's bright-red robe. It looked like someone had splashed blood all over the computer screen.

Louie stopped short. Max bumped right into him and fell to the ground with a thud. The camera tilted upward so that all you could see was the inside of Louie's nose.

George laughed. There was **a big booger** up there.

"You can't come in the bathroom with me!" Louie shouted at Max. "Just stay out here, and I'll sing really loud." And with that, he slammed the door.

Now all George could see was a bathroom door. And all he could hear was Louie screeching out his favorite song.

"Louie, Louie . . . oh no. We gotta go. Aye-yi-yi-yi . . ."

George clicked off the computer screen. There was only so much a guy could take.

"Nice shower cap, Louie," George said as he, Alex, and Chris met up with the other kids in the schoolyard the next morning.

Louie glared at George. "I have a very dry scalp," he said. "If I wash my hair every day, I'll get **dandruff**."

"Why did you take a shower in the middle of your show, anyway?" Julianna asked him. "No one could see you."

"But you could *hear* me," Louie said. "That was the whole point. And you could see me before I went into the bathroom." He glared at George. "*My whole face.* Not just my hand."

"Oh yeah," Alex said. "We saw all of you. **Including your nostrils.**"

George laughed. "You got a lot of hair

up there," he said. "And other stuff, too . . . *achoo!*"

Alex and George laughed. So did Chris, Julianna, and Sage. Max and Mike started to, but one look from Louie stopped them cold.

George thought about making another crack about Louie's shower cap and nose hairs. But he stopped himself. That just wasn't something the new and improved George would do. Besides, the kids had more important things to think about than *Life with Louie*.

"I'm going to wait in line outside the TV station right after school," George said. "Mrs. Kelly is sure to dance better if she knows **people are rooting for her**. My dad is driving me over. Anyone need a ride?"

"I do," Alex said.

"I'll go with you, George," Chris added.

"Me too," Julianna said. "My parents are out of town again, and my grandmother's car smells really gross."

"I'll ride with you, too, *Georgie*," Sage said. "I can sit next to you. Or **on your lap** if there isn't room in the car."

No way *that* was happening. "My dad's bringing the van. You'll have your own seat," George told Sage. Then he walked away as fast as he could.

"Oh man, stuck in a van with Sage," George complained as he and Alex hurried into the school building. "I sure hope this is gonna be worth it."

"It will be," Alex said. "It's a scientific fact that people do better when they know there are people cheering them on. So the more people who cheer, and the louder we do it, the better Mrs. Kelly will dance. And the better chance she'll have at winning."

George grinned. He really wanted Mrs. Kelly to win. It would be so amazing to have a teacher who was a real live *superstar*!

Chapter 9

"This place is a lot smaller than it looks on TV," George said as he took his seat in the *Dance Your Pants Off* studio later that day. "I'm glad we got here early. We never would have gotten a seat."

"But now we're **right down in front**," Chris said. "We'll see everything!"

Alex nodded. Then he bent down and reached under his seat. "Check it out!" he said, holding up a piece of hard, green gum. "A new piece of already been chewed gum to add to my gum ball!"

George smiled. "That's gotta be a good sign," he told Alex. "Maybe that

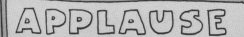

gum will bring Mrs. Kelly luck!"

"*I* can't believe I had to postpone my *Life with Louie* broadcast for this," Louie groaned. "I was all ready to talk about cheese from around the world. My mom said I could use her sterling silver cheese slicer and everything."

"That would have been interesting," Max agreed. "Louie knows a lot about cheese."

"Yeah, **no one's more cheesy than you, Louie**," Mike added.

George laughed. "That's for sure."

"There wouldn't have been anyone home to watch it, anyway," Julianna reminded Louie. "Practically the whole fourth grade is *here*."

"I know. That's why I decided to come instead of doing my show," Louie agreed. "I'll do a new *Life with Louie* tomorrow. No one would want to miss my discussion of the difference between Roquefort and blue cheese."

"Who cares what the difference is?" George groaned. "**They both stink!** My grandmother once made me a blue cheese omelet. It smelled like feet."

"How much longer until the show starts?" Chris asked.

"About twenty minutes," Alex said, looking at his watch.

"Oh, man," Chris groaned. "That's a long time to just sit here."

George knew what Chris meant. He had a tough time sitting still, too.

Bing-bong . . .

And it was about to get even tougher. Because just then, George felt something that never sat still. Ever.

Cling-clang!

Ping-pong!

The super burp was back! And it

wanted to play. Already the bubbles were bing-bonging on his bladder and doing **loop-the-loops** on his liver.

George wanted to give Alex their secret signal. But Alex was looking the other way and talking to Julianna.

Now the bubbles were using George's tongue as a trampoline. *Boing! Boing! Boing!*

"Georgie, are you okay?" Sage asked him. "Your eyes are bulging."

George let out the loudest burp anyone had ever heard. The whole audience stared at him.

"Georgie!" Sage shouted, surprised.

George opened his mouth to say

"excuse me." But that's not what came out. Instead, George's mouth shouted, "I'VE GOT BOOGIE FEVER!"

The next thing anyone knew, George's feet were **dancing their way down the aisle** of the *Dance Your Pants Off* studio and climbing the steps to the stage.

The audience started to laugh!

"Kid! Get down from there!" one of the stagehands shouted.

But George's feet weren't going anywhere. The super burp had never met a stage it didn't love.

George's body started dancing. His rear end gave a wiggle, and his belly gave a jiggle. Then he kicked his right leg in and his left leg out.

The audience members laughed even louder.

"Oh man, George is in trouble now!" Louie shouted over all the laughter.

George hated being in trouble. But the burp didn't mind at all. *Trouble* was the super burp's middle name—or it would have been if **magical super burps** had middle names.

"Dude!" Alex shouted. He ran for the stage.

"Kid, you can't be up there, either!" the stagehand shouted at Alex.

George's legs kicked higher and higher.

Alex reached over and **grabbed George by the pant leg**.

Bam! George tripped and landed right on his behind. But his rear end didn't mind. It started spinning on the stage, taking Alex with it.

Alex tugged hard, trying to get George off the stage. But the burp was in charge of George now. And it wasn't going anywhere. George stood up and started doing the Watusi.

Yank! Alex tugged even harder on George's pant leg.

Oops. **The pants slid off** George's waist and fell down around his ankles.

Whoosh! Just then, George felt something *pop* inside his belly. All the air rushed out of him. The super burp was gone!

But George was right there, standing in the middle of the stage, in front of the whole studio audience, *in his tighty whities*!

Everyone in the audience was laughing and pointing right at George. This was a nightmare.

Just then, Guy Smirks walked onto the stage. He stared at George and Alex.

"Oh, man, **he's gonna get it now**." Louie laughed. "They're gonna throw that weirdo freak right out of here!"

George frowned. Louie was right. He was definitely getting thrown out of here now. He was going to miss the whole show. And Alex probably would, too. Which wasn't fair. He'd just been trying to keep George out of trouble.

Guy smiled out at the audience. "Now *that's* what I call dancing your pants off!" The audience **cheered wildly**.

"Good job, kid," Guy said, wrapping his arm around George. "You've gotten this audience really warmed up. They're in a great mood! And that makes for great TV."

George didn't know what to say. He **just stood there**, listening to the audience cheer.

"But maybe you should pull your pants up," Guy reminded him.

George blushed. He bent down and **pulled his pants back up**.

"Let's give these two kids one more cheer," Guy said.

"WOO-HOO!" The audience members all shouted, clapped, and stomped their feet. Well, almost all of the audience members, anyway. Louie was just sitting there, staring at the stage. He couldn't believe this was happening.

"Now you kids better go sit down," Guy told George and Alex. "The show's about to start." He laughed. "Although I'm pretty sure none of these dancers are ever going to be able to top that!"

Chapter 10

"Is it on yet?" George asked as he flopped down in front of the living room couch on Friday night at eight o'clock.

"It's starting now," his dad said.

"I sure hope Mrs. Kelly got enough votes to go through to the next round," George said, although he doubted it. Mrs. Kelly's dance on last night's show had been **horrible**. She'd done some weird spinning around on her back, then jumped up, wiggled her hips, and taken a flying leap across the stage. Mrs. Kelly had described her dance as a hip-hop, hula, and ballet combination. But to George, it just looked like a crazy mess.

"Welcome to the *Dance Your Pants Off* Results Show!" Guy Smirks shouted into the camera. "Tonight we'll find out if your favorite dancer will make it through to next week's show." He held up an envelope. "I've got the results right here!"

George crossed his fingers. He crossed his toes. He tried to cross his eyes, but then the TV screen looked all fuzzy.

"Okay, the **first dancer to be safe tonight is**"—Guy Smirks looked into the camera and ever so slowly opened the envelope. George held his breath.— "Sergio Smith!"

The spotlight fell on a man in a pair of black pants and a white shirt. Sergio took a bow and walked off the stage.

"I didn't think he was so good," George said.

But he had been a better dancer than Mrs. Kelly. So had the next three

dancers—Elise, Marsha, and Ricky—who
were all moving on to the next round.
By the time the commercial break came,
there were only two dancers left:
Mrs. Kelly and some lady named Casey,
who had done a cartwheel in the middle
of her dance and landed right on her rear
end. That had to have cost her some votes.
Maybe Mrs. Kelly did have a chance.

"Okay, Mildred and Casey," Guy
Smirks said when the commercial ended.
"It's down to the two of you. One of you
will be dancing next week, and one of
you will be going home. The person
who received the most votes and will be
staying is . . ."

George was **sweating all over**. His
heart was pounding. His fingers and toes
were cramped from being crossed for so
long. "Mrs. Kelly," he whispered. "Mrs.
Kelly . . ."

"Casey!" Guy Smirks announced. He turned to Mrs. Kelly. "Mildred, that means you're going home. I'm sorry."

Mrs. Kelly looked like she was going to cry. Her face was all red, and her eyes were glassy. George turned away. He didn't want to watch his teacher cry on TV. That would just make seeing her on Monday **waaaaayyy too bizarre**.

"Shh . . . I think I hear her coming," Julianna whispered to the other kids in class 401 on

Monday morning. They had all arrived very early that morning and beaten their teacher to the classroom.

Mrs. Kelly walked inside and flicked on the lights.

"Surprise!" the kids shouted as they **threw confetti in the air**.

Sage flicked on the MP3 player. *"Walk like an Egyptian!"* she shouted as the music played.

And then the kids all began to dance around the room, just like Mrs. Kelly had taught them. George knew they looked **ridiculous**. But Mrs. Kelly seemed really happy. She pulled out a wrinkled tissue that was tucked in her sleeve and wiped her eyes.

Sage and Julianna danced over to their teacher. They were carrying a small plastic trophy.

"You're the champion dancer here at Edith B. Sugarman Elementary School!" Julianna told Mrs. Kelly.

Mrs. Kelly wiped her eyes again and smiled. "Well, what are you all standing around here for?" she asked. **"Let's dance our pants off!"** Mrs. Kelly looked at George and laughed. "I didn't mean that literally, George," she teased. "You should definitely keep *your* pants on!"

The kids all laughed. Louie laughed louder than anyone!

George felt his face turning red. He was never going to forget how embarrassing it had been standing there in front of a whole studio audience in his tighty whities.

Just then, George felt something weird inside him. Really weird. Like he was being **tickled from the inside**. He gulped. Oh no! Not again! Not the . . .

ACHOO!

Phew! It had only been a sneeze. A big, gooey, watery sneeze, for sure. But *just* a sneeze. And that was good news. Because sneezes might bring boogers, but they didn't bring trouble.

George smiled and moved his head back and forth like an ancient Egyptian. "Let's dance!" he cried out happily.

Chapter 11

"You better not act goofy tonight," Louie said as George walked into Louie's mansion a few weeks later. "My mom said I had to invite everyone in the class to watch the finale of *Dance Your Pants Off*. But she's definitely gonna be **keeping her eye on you**."

George frowned. Mrs. Farley had hated George ever since the super burp had made him go all crazy at Louie's birthday party last summer, at the spring talent show, at the fall spelling bee, and while the kids were caroling on her lawn last Christmas. The super burp was a burp for all seasons. And that made grown-ups like Mrs. Farley nuts.

"Here you go, Georgie," Sage said. "I saved you a seat right next to me."

There was no way George was sitting next to Sage. He plopped down on the floor next to Alex.

"Hey, dude," Alex said. "Check out that TV."

George looked up at the **massive flat-screen TV** in the middle of Louie's living room. It was as huge as a movie theater screen.

"This is going to be awesome," George said. "Even if it *is* at Louie's house."

"Okay, everyone be quiet," Louie said. "The show is starting."

"Welcome to the *Dance Your Pants Off* Finale!" Guy Smirks announced. "It's been quite a season. Before we get to the final performances, let's take a look back at the dances we've seen so far."

One by one, past dancers flashed across

the screen. When Mrs. Kelly came on doing her hip-hop hula, the kids all cheered.

And then . . . suddenly . . . *someone else* appeared on the TV screen.

"George! What are you doing on TV?" Louie shouted angrily.

Sure enough, there was George, dancing his pants off—literally. Everyone in the room cheered louder. Well, everyone except Louie, Max, and Mike, anyway.

"Wow, dude!" Alex said excitedly.

"My mom and dad gave them permission to show the tape of me dancing that night," George explained proudly.

"Georgie, you're a TV star!" Sage said.

"No, he's not!" Louie insisted. "*I'm* the star. I'm the one with my own show! *Life with Louie,* remember?"

Sure, everyone remembered, but no one cared. For now, the only star in the room was George Brown. Well, actually, it was

George's super burp that was the real star.
But there was no way George was giving
that burp any credit for anything. Not now.
Not ever!

About the Author

Nancy Krulik is the author of more than 150 books for children and young adults including three *New York Times* best sellers and the popular Katie Kazoo, Switcheroo books. She lives in New York City with her family, and many of George Brown's escapades are based on things her own kids have done. (No one delivers a good burp quite like Nancy's son, Ian!) Nancy's favorite thing to do is laugh, which comes in pretty handy when you're trying to write funny books!

About the Illustrator

Aaron Blecha was raised by a school of giant squid in Wisconsin and now lives with his family by the English seaside. He works as an artist designing toys, animating cartoons, and illustrating books, including the Zombiekins and The Rotten Adventures of Zachary Ruthless series. You can enjoy more of his weird creations at www.monstersquid.com.